painted love letters

Catherine Bateson grew up in a secondhand bookshop in Brisbane — an ideal childhood for a writer. She has written two collections of poetry and two verse novels for young adults, *A Dangerous Girl* and its sequel, *The Year It All Happened*. Catherine lives in Central Victoria with her husband and their two children. She has taught creative writing for over a decade and particularly likes conducting writing workshops in schools. This is Catherine's first prose novel.

Poetry
The Vigilant Heart

For Young Adults
A Dangerous Girl
The Year It All Happened

painted
love
letters

catherine bateson

University of Queensland Press

First published 2002 by University of Queensland Press
Box 6042, St Lucia, Queensland 4067 Australia

www.uqp.uq.edu.au

Typeset by University of Queensland Press
Printed in Australia by McPherson's Printing Group

Distributed in the USA and Canada by
International Specialized Book Services, Inc.,
5824 N.E. Hassalo Street, Portland, Oregon 97213–3640

Cataloguing in Publication Data
National Library of Australia

Bateson, Catherine.
   Painted love letters.

   I. Title.

A823.4

ISBN 0 7022 3289 0

In Memory Of
Ronald G. Campbell 1898–1970
Mal Morgan 1935–1999

With many thanks to Varuna — The Writers' House for their invaluable mentorship program, to my fellow participants and with particular gratitude to Hazel Edwards, a generous and inspiring mentor.

Contents

1   Before and After   *1*

2   Love Letters and Coffins   *12*

3   Oysters   *25*

4   Nan and Badger   *41*

5   Leprosy, Leonardo and Father Damien   *61*

6   Unfinished Business   *72*

7   The Bougainvillea   *84*

Before and After

Dad said that in Nurralloo we were surrounded by Philistines who wouldn't know a good painting if it jumped up and bit them, but at the pub they hung one of his small watercolours; a sketch he called it, and Dad got free beers. He said by the time I was sixteen, we'd be rich. We'd celebrate my birthday in Paris, the city of art and lovers. Mum said, 'Don't put ideas in her head, Dave Grainger. Chrissie, don't listen to him,' and flicked her tea towel at him but later she pulled down one of Dad's art books and showed me paintings of people dancing in Paris and a Paris pub which looked a lot posher than the Station Hotel.

I didn't want to go to Paris, even though the pictures looked nice. We'd only been in Nurralloo for one-and-a-half-years. I'd had to change schools halfway through the year and explain to everyone all over again that my father was an artist and that's why he stayed at home and didn't work like the other dads, driving trucks for the council or farming. I've already been in three schools and lived in one city, one big town, seven houses, one flat and a caravan park since I was born.

When I couldn't sleep I used to lie in bed counting them on my fingers and trying to remember each place. I couldn't remember the first couple of houses of course, because I was just a baby. The first place I could really remember was Nan's in Sydney. There was a pale couch and I was never ever to put my feet on it. I had to wipe my dirty shoes on a mat that said WELCOME at the front door with a cat curled up under the words. Dad said the mat was false advertising.

Then I can remember a caravan park somewhere — it was actually in New South Wales but I can't remember the drive to get there or anything except the walking to the toilet block in the night and how it was kind of scary but kind of nice and once we saw a possum. And you had to have a shower, not a bath. Then the flat — but all I can remember is watching the television and a big fight between Mum and Dad. The flat was too small, Mum said, your father couldn't work and he was very unhappy. Then there were two or three houses edging up the New South Wales Coast towards Queensland — I get them mixed up because we didn't stay in any of them very long. Then we did this jump — Dad showed me on the map — and ended up in Taylor Street,

Toowoomba where Dad went off to work nearly every day.

I remember Taylor Street because I started school while we lived there and went right through Grade One and nearly all the way through Mrs Dean's Second Grade. There were roses in the front garden, lots of them. I had my photo taken by one of Dad's friends who taught with him out at the college. He taught photography and my father taught print-making. And I got a brand new bike with a little purple basket for my birthday. I kept the bike even though it is too little for me to ride anymore. I kept it in case Mum had another baby and she nearly did, but something went wrong and it was born too early.

Then we moved outside Toowoomba and Dad stopped going to work every day although he still drove in a couple of times a week. I didn't have to finish that year at school because it would have been a waste of time. Mum and Dad argued again but it wasn't because he didn't have a studio. And Mum sat in the dark a lot, or hugged me so tightly I couldn't breathe. It had to do with the baby but I didn't like it much, although I knew I had to stay very still and let her do it.

Then, we moved to Nurralloo and I had to start all over again, but this is the best house we've ever lived in because we've got a dog called Bongo, Dad's got a studio-shed, Mum's got her own room to dream in and I've got a bedroom with a door on to the verandah which means I can go and look at the stars at night. One day, when I know enough stars, I'm going to count them, instead of the places I've lived. They've got nicer names, although they're harder to say.

These were the things you could rely on in Nurralloo, where we lived: fresh eggs every day from Mum's chooks, Stinge McPhee's early Saturday visit before he drove to Toowoomba for the races and Dad's morning ritual. He would get up, cough his guts up, make some Nescafe, sit on the front door step and light his first cigarette. My father smoked Camel cigarettes, or roll your owns when we ran out of money.

I didn't want to go to Paris, even though it is the most beautiful city in the world and the city of love, or *lerv* as Mum says, rolling her eyes. I didn't want to go anywhere. Nurralloo suited me fine. So when I heard Mum say, 'Well that's it, Dave, if Dr. Gregg says to get a second opinion, we'll go to the city,' my heart slid right out of my chest and made it down to the toes of my boots. I sprang out of my room quicker than Bongo bounds after a rabbit.

They were standing on opposite sides of the kitchen table. Mum's face was floury. She'd been making bread. The flour made dusty patches on her face and when she pushed her hair away, the flour clung there, too, making her look grey.

'It's probably nothing,' Dad said, 'he just wants me to have a couple of tests. He said it's probably just a really persistent bug but that I should have an X-ray, just in case. He wants to make sure my lungs are clear. There's no drama, Rhetta. There's no need to pack up and drive all the way to the city. We can do this in Toowoomba. Please don't turn into your mother over this.'

He sounded tired when he said that, and, for a minute when I looked at him he didn't seem like my father anymore, just a man who looked sick and grey and I was shocked and wanted to be back reading on my bed with Bongo sleeping on the end but it was too late. I was stuck in the kitchen, watching them and listening.

We drove back from Brisbane city the day after the seventeen men were killed in Ipswich in an explosion at the Box Flat coal mine. Fourteen men were sealed in the mine. Mum said they were already dead but it didn't matter, it didn't matter one little bit to me because my father had lung cancer. He had X-rays to prove it and a cough that wouldn't go away ever now. Mum drove all the way home, wiping the tears off her face and no-one said anything much because what was there to say? When we drove through Ipswich my mother said, 'Those poor men, those poor families left behind, wondering.' And then she sniffed extra loudly and we drove on in silence.

Dad reached for his cigarettes every so often and then stopped and his hands returned to rest in his lap. Sometimes I snuck my hand in with his and then he'd stroke my knuckles or we'd hold each other's hands until they got too hot and sweaty. The ute rattled on to Toowoomba but we didn't want to eat so Mum drove on out of town and made us eat hamburgers and chips at the truck stop, even though we'd been vegetarians for years.

Normally I would have loved it, the salty hot fat chips, the grey meat, the surprising wickedness of it. Just as I had loved watching the television in the hotel room in Brisbane and Mum not even saying to turn it off but sitting there with me, watching anything, everything. Even "Number 96" which she hated. But that was before we knew, that was before the tests came through and now everything, even hot chips, would taste the same; dust or clouds, which, like medicine, you had to take.

Mum and I kept looking at Dad who fiddled with his paper napkin and didn't eat much. He'd clear his throat as if to say something and end up coughing and then Mum would look scared. I was angry — it wasn't as if he always didn't cough. There was nothing new except that now he was dying even though Mum said that wasn't true, he wasn't necessarily dying there were things they could do. But then why did we all have to act as though he was and why did we have to move because that's what we were going to do? We were going back to Nurralloo to move to Brisbane because that way Dad would have a fighting chance, Mum said.

'So much for country living,' she said, days later, throwing clothes in a suitcase, 'so much for the healthy air, home produce and all the rest of the crap. I just wish, I just wish ...'

She didn't finish the sentence and I could think of only one thing she would wish for, the one thing that silenced us, so I didn't even ask, but went on piling the books in the cartons.

People kept coming round. More people came round than I thought we really knew. They brought empty boxes, casseroles full of chops, a plate of roast lamb, a lemon meringue pie. They brought their own stories of cancer and told them in the kitchen while they made pots of tea and my mother kept packing.

'Remember Lizzie, or Dawn, or Pam,' they'd say and then there'd be a story about a breast that had to come off or another bit of someone that was removed. Most of the stories would end with the person getting better and going on to win money at the races, or First Prize for fruit cake at the Toowoomba Show. And they'd pat Mum on the back and pour another cuppa.

At school it was different. The kids had stories too. Someone's uncle had been sliced open and there it was, right through him. All they could do was sew him up again and send him home to lie in bed until he died.

'He was riddled with it,' Jacko said, smacking his lips, 'positively riddled with it.'

I had seen highway signs riddled with bullet holes and I wondered if my father's lungs looked like that, shot with lots of little holes. No wonder he couldn't breathe properly, the oxygen would go straight through those holes.

I left Nurralloo before third term properly finished. I unclipped my paintings from the lines and packed away my unfinished space project. My best friend, Lynnette Graham, hugged me, promised she'd write and even began to cry before her mother gently untangled us and led her away.

Mum promised me the new house was great — I would have a terrific bedroom, she said. I would be able to decorate it any way I liked. The back yard was huge, she said, big enough for any games I played. It wasn't, though, it wasn't the acres we had, with Mr Evan's cows. And my bedroom wasn't off a verandah. I could either have the middle room, which had no window at all, only a door leading to the sleep-out, or I could sleep in the sleep-out which wasn't a proper bedroom at all and the bathroom was just off it so I could hear the toilet flushing in the night.

'It was the best house available,' Mum said, sharply, 'close to everything; shops, the school, the hospital, so just shut up and unpack your stuff wherever you're going to sleep.'

'Rhetta,' Dad said, coming in, 'please, please.'

Please what? I wondered, but I didn't ask any more questions. I had heard what mattered. We were close to the hospital.

'Look, Chrissie,' Dad said later that night, when we drove to Kentucky Fried Chicken to get the family special — which we never would have eaten before. Mum wouldn't have let us. She didn't believe the stories about them using rats but she hated battery hens. 'The river's just down there. We'll be able to take Bongo down there for walks. And there are different things to do in the city, you'll see.'

After dinner I went into the sleep-out and stared around it. Yes, it was my same bed with the shelf for books on the bedhead. Yes, they were the same sheets, the pale blue ones with clouds and birds flying through them and a matching pillow case. Yes, my books were on the bookshelf and my ornaments, photos and hairbrush on the dressing table, and my dressing gown hung on a hook behind the door. Bongo had made his place on the bottom of the bed but even he looked dejected. His black and white tail gave only one distinct thump as I tucked myself in, careful to move my feet around him. I stared up at the ceiling and could think of nothing good about this new place except that it was close to the hospital. That was all.

When my father first told my mother the news, she had sat in the fluro light of the hotel room,

on the edge of the bed and banged her fist on
the blue chenille bedspread and said the 'f' word.
Not once, but three times, as hard and fast as
the bullets some gangster was shooting on the
television screen. I had never before heard her
say that word but now I knew how you could
want to shock the world, the universe, with
some hard ugliness of your own, when everything seemed to be so wrong, so utterly wrong
and you had run out of hope for it ever getting
better.

I wondered if the men in the mine had banged
their dirty fists against the rock and yelled out
the 'f' word or whether they had turned and held
each other, tenderly, the way people do in movies when bad news is delivered or disasters
happen. Perhaps they had only had time to look
at each other, mouths open like hooked fish,
before the explosion blasted them to kingdom
come.

I stared up at the ceiling and could think of
nothing good in the whole world and I said the
worst thing I could think. I said, 'I hate you God'.
And I thought of my mother's fists and the dust
motes rising from the bedspread and I said, 'F
you'.

No fiery blast or thundery voice crashed from
the clouds. Just nothing. The room was silent
except for Bongo whimpering a little as he
dreamed of the Nurralloo rabbits. Well, what had
I expected? I didn't have that much to do with

God, we didn't go to church at all, so he hadn't recognised my voice. Then I dragged Bongo up next to me and wrapped my arms around his shaggy, obliging chest. He smelled grottily alive, a good thick smell as comforting as soup.

Love Letters and Coffins

 Dad was obsessed with the cost of funerals. He talked about it all the time. He wrote letters to the newspapers about it. One was published in *The Courier-Mail* and I hoped no-one at school saw it. Dad cut the letter out and stuck it on the notice board in our kitchen, right next to the card notifying him of his next hospital appointment.

Everything he didn't want, he made me write down in a notebook. He didn't want a mahogany coffin, red or white satin lining, brass or silver-plated handles and he particularly didn't want flowers.

'Tell everyone to donate the money they would have spent on wreaths to cancer research,' he said, and I wrote it down.

He didn't want: a multinational funeral home taking care of his remains, strangers saying anything at his funeral, and he particularly didn't want to be buried.

'Cremation. Wrap me in a plain shroud and cremate me.' he said.

'What's a shroud?' I asked, 'and how do you spell it?'

I wrote it down. I had a list of what he wanted and a list of what he didn't want.

'I don't want you remembering me as a sick old man,' he said, but I didn't have to write that down.

'I don't want my death mourned, I want my life celebrated,' he said. I didn't write that down.

'You can't make us not feel sad,' I said, 'it doesn't work that way, Dad.' Then I had to leave the room because he also didn't want anyone to cry.

'It's so unfair,' I said to my mother when she got home from work. 'It's all right for him to say what he wants and doesn't want. He'll be dead. What about us? What about what we want?'

Mum pulled me into her white shirt. She smelled of kitchens, oil and steam. She was waitressing at the Queen Victoria Hotel. She was a bistro girl, she told our friends, grimacing.

'The thing is, Chrissie, that when you're very, very sick like Dad is, you don't always have the energy to think about other people. I know it seems unfair, but that's how it is. Do you want me to talk to him?'

I thought about it. After each bout of chemotherapy my father came home looking greyer and as though there was a little less of him.

'No,' I said, 'don't bother.'

Dad talked to some friends of his and found a carpenter who agreed to come around and measure him up. The carpenter was a thin, long man with greying dreadlocks who didn't comment on Dad's stash of illegal pain relief, the dope he smoked throughout the day.

'Cool, man,' Bodhi kept saying as he flicked his carpenter's rule at my father's body. 'So what do you reckon, recycled timber or you got something else in mind?'

'I don't care, Bodhi, the cheapest thing you can get. I don't care if it's plywood.'

'Plywood wouldn't hold you,' Bodhi said, 'I'll get hunting. Tell you what, let me measure up your old woman and I'll give you a cheaper deal for two.'

'That's a great idea,' Dad said, pouring Bodhi out some lemon grass tea, and filling the bong, 'that way I could paint Rhetta's too while I'm still around.'

'Right,' Bodhi nodded his head so emphatically his dreadlocks bounced around like little snakes, 'like, it would be there when she needed it.'

'Dad,' I said, 'Dad, I don't know if that's such a great idea.'

I could tell that it was too late.

'What about the kid?'

'No way,' I said.

'Not Chrissie,' Dad said, 'we don't even know how tall she'll get.'

'What I want,' I said, 'are flowers at the funeral.'

'Flowers are pretty,' Bodhi said, setting his snakes dancing again.

'Waste of money,' Dad said. 'We can paint flowers on the coffin.'

'I only want my bunch.'

It felt to me that a funeral wasn't a funeral without one bunch of flowers, just like a wedding wouldn't be a wedding. Or maybe I had a picture of myself laying the flowers gently on the coffin. I could see the bunch of flowers, kind of pathetic, kind of brave. Which was how I felt most of the time. The flowers and my hand were the only things I could see. I couldn't imagine how my father would go from discussing the coffin with Bodhi to actually lying in it, not breathing any more.

'A little bunch wouldn't hurt,' Bodhi said. 'She's just a kid, Davo, give her a little bunch of flowers, man, they're not going to change the world. You've got to flow with these things, you've got to know that while you're the main dude in all this, it's the old woman's and the kid's gig. You won't be there for the final party, man.'

'Okay, okay,' Dad said. 'Get the book, Chrissie.' I fetched the funeral book and I crossed out 'no flowers' and put in 'Chrissie's flowers only.'

'Cool,' Bodhi said examining the notebook, 'fantastic idea, man. I reckon these should be marketed. Everyone should have a funeral plan. My old woman had a birth plan, you know, for when Tibet came along. But it all went to hell. Sari just couldn't embrace the pain. Now, when do you want these by?'

'Soon,' Dad said grimacing, 'make it sooner, rather than later.'

'It's a deal. I'll start getting them knocked up right away.'

It didn't take Bodhi long — he delivered two new coffins to our house within a couple of weeks. They came just before I left for school one morning and Dad went out to take delivery, wearing a new plaid dressing gown. This time a year ago, he'd have just wrapped himself in one of Mum's sarongs and sauntered out, a cup of tea steaming in one hand, a cigarette burning in the other.

Bodhi and his mate put the coffins in the shed where Mum had let me put up a table tennis table we'd bought cheaply at a farm clearance sale. It sat there, unused. I felt it called a still-unknown friend to me. But the coffins went on the table tennis table. Dad ran a finger along the surface. 'Great,' he said, and, 'like the handles.'

The handles were made from heavy rope and the coffin itself was a pale untreated pine. I had not wanted to see them arrive. I had rather hoped that Bodhi would turn out to be unreliable and the coffins would never arrive. If I thought of coffins, along with my hand, and the bunch of flowers, I saw something dark and lustrous, like a grand piano. That was the kind I expected.

'Well there you are, Davo, I'm thinking of advertising them, you know. So when you get them painted, give us a tinkle and I'll come over with the camera, if you don't mind.'

'Not at all,' Dad said, 'In fact, if they look okay, I'll put them in the show that's coming up, if … well if.'

'Yeah, sure. Great idea, man. Embrace it, Davo, embrace it.'

Dad started painting that morning. I got to school late because I had to help him set up. Not that I told anyone that. I was just beginning to find my way around the city school and I didn't want weird stories about my family spoiling things.

Still, I was curious, so the first thing I did when I got home was check out the coffin. Dad had already painted the sides in an abstract pattern of what could have almost been footprints, footprints in water, though, not sand or earth. It was good. You could look at it and know it was David Grainger's work, the way you have to with art. They were the same colours he used in his etchings, and with the same kind of shapes that made you think of real things, even though they themselves weren't what had been painted.

'What do you think? Do you like it?' Dad asked that evening.

'Yeah, yeah I do,' I said. 'I reckon it's coming along well.'

He did the top next, sort of stick figures in a big space of green moving into red, moving into black, so that I thought of how when you live in the country the sky's always huge and the stars don't go anywhere near filling all that darkness. The coffin reminded me of how small I'd felt looking up at the country sky and I knew those figures, if they were people, felt the same way about the colours Dad had used. They were so big and deep they overwhelmed the little clay-coloured dots and dashes who might have been walking through them.

The painting made me cry in the night. It made me wish we were the kind of family who went to church. I wanted to say a prayer to a god somewhere, but I didn't know how, and I didn't feel I could ask either Mum or Dad what you did about that.

Instead I asked Dee Browning at school. Dee wasn't my friend or anything. She was just this girl I hung around with even though I wasn't sure I liked her. She was bigger and older than me. She'd been kept down, not once, but twice. The teachers said Dee was slow, although she looked fast and sharp in her leather-look mini and her nearly high-heeled sandals. Dee went to church, I knew, because she wore a little silver medal of the Virgin Mary cradling a bundle which was the baby Jesus.

'Dee, can anyone go to your church?' I asked at snack time. We were standing on the edge of the oval and Dee was watching the boys pass a football back and forth. 'You know, suppose you weren't really sure what you were, could you just kind of front up and they'd let you in?'

Dee looked down at me. She had a way of doing that. It made me feel small and drab. She blinked and her eyelashes fluttered blue.

'Well, of course, Chrissie, the church is open to all Jesus's little children.'

'Yeah, but what about me?'

'You? I don't know about you. Have you been christened?'

I shook my head. I wasn't really sure, but it seemed unlikely.

'Well, I'd have to ask my mother, but I don't think they'd kick you out.'

Dad started on Mum's coffin. It was really different. Though the same things were there, 'motifs', Dad said, the footsteps didn't walk though, they skipped through a yellow-pink-ness as though they were dancing. The colour reminded me of the roses from one of the gardens we'd had. When I told Dad he nodded in a pleased way.

'Taylor Street,' he said, 'your mum loved that garden.'

Dee said that I could go to church with her that Sunday if I wanted but I'd have to be up early, and then afterwards I could go home with her for Sunday lunch. Her mum made roast lamb, she said, and her sisters came with their babies. It was not something I would normally feel comfortable doing but it seemed to be part of the same deal, so I asked Mum, leaving out the church business and she said yes, of course. I felt bad because she was pleased I'd made a friend and Dee wasn't quite that.

For the top of Mum's coffin, Dad used gold paint and the little dots and dashes from his coffin had become swirling letters, except you couldn't read what they said, they just swirled and looped as though you should be able to. It was so beautiful it made my whole chest ache and, although I didn't really want to look at it, a part of me couldn't stop — like overhearing a conversation you shouldn't listen to, but your feet won't move you away and down the hall. It was a love letter my father had written to my mother, and only she'd be able to read it properly.

I didn't tell Mum that when I found her crying in the kitchen, holding a tea towel over her mouth. I didn't tell her because she said she was crying because she'd burnt her hand at work, and when I looked, the burn was there, a large welt across her wrist. I found the first aid kit and put burn cream on it for her and we didn't talk about the coffins in the shed.

I went to church with Dee, her mother and her little brother. I got up when they got up, I knelt down when they knelt down, I shared Dee's Bible and her hymn book and I watched her whole family go to the front of the church for Communion. I said sorry to God for what I had said when we first came to Brisbane, that first night. And then I tried to pray, not just for Dad but the fourteen men sealed under the Box Flat coal mine, and their kids if they had any. It didn't make me feel better. Maybe you had to practise to get it right.

I managed to answer all Mrs Browning's questions over lunch without once saying about Dad's cancer. I talked about his exhibition and made it sound like we'd moved from the country to the city so he could work on it. I made everything sound pink and yellow. I saw myself in a mirror that hung on their dining room wall, and I looked smoothed out and rosy, as though I were a completely different person.

Later, Dee walked me home. She wanted to see my bedroom but I knew it wouldn't interest her when she saw it. I didn't have posters of pop groups stuck on the walls. I didn't have an autographed photo of anyone from any televison programme, and my wardrobe couldn't rival her collection of mini skirts and little bubble tops.

So I took her into the backyard where at least there was the mango tree to climb. She wouldn't though, because she didn't want to scratch her legs, so I thought of the only other thing I could offer.

'Table tennis?'

'Oh yeah. That'd be neat. I haven't played table tennis since we went on holidays. I was really good at it,' Dee replied.

I opened the shed door and remembered. The coffins were both finished, side by side on the table in full sight.

Dee took a step forward and then stopped, her eyes widening.

'Maybe it isn't such a great idea,' I said desperately, 'we could do something else.'

It was too late.

Dee shrieked a cockatoo shriek and then she turned on me, 'Are you the Addams family or something! That's disgusting! You must be vampires. Who's in them, Chrissie, who's in them? Can I have a closer look?'

'No.' I said, pushing at her to get her out of the shed, 'No. My father doesn't like people looking at them. He's an artist, I told you. It's just a new line of work.'

'That's so spooky. I bet you dream of them at night. I bet you dream of vampires coming to get you. I couldn't sleep if I were you. Not with vampires and coffins in the shed. God, it's so gruesome. Can I have a proper look?'

'No,' I managed to shove her right out and then

I shut the door. 'I think you'd better go home now Dee, there's nothing to do round here, anyway.'

'I'm going all right. I don't want to hang round with a freaky vampire. You might bite my neck,' and she tilted her head as though to offer me a better look at her long, tanned neck.

'Yeah,' I said, 'watch out!' and I lunged at her, baring my teeth.

She told the whole class. I knew she would. I'd have told if I'd been her. All I could do was lift my head a little higher and try not to look like the kind of girl who would have coffins in her shed, even though I was from the country and my father was an artist. I said in the clear confident voice Dad had taught me to use for bluffing at poker, that Dee was saying that just because she'd lost at table tennis and wasn't that typical. She was such a poor loser and spiteful. And I looked at them with my best bluffer's face.

'Who'd keep coffins in a shed?' I said, and shook my head, 'Gosh, Dee, what have you been smoking?'

I told Dee in front of everyone that lying was a sin, and she should know she'd go to Hell and burn forever. I said if you wanted gruesome, you should see the picture Dee had in her kitchen of Jesus with his chest open and blood seeping down.

We fought it out on the tan bark, scratching,

kicking and pulling each other's hair with the rest of the kids cheering us on until Mr Chapman came and broke it up. My face looked as though I'd put it too close to a feral cat but Dee's top lip was already swelling. As we were hauled off to the headmaster's office I looked down at my still clenched right hand and I wanted to shout a big victory whoop, high and wild enough to crack the windows. It was so good to feel my reliable heart pumping and my clean lungs grabbing all that good air.

Oysters

 I couldn't do art at my new school the summer my father lay on the couch, slowly dying. I went to class and I dabbed away at sponge paintings, had a go at monoprints and I drew the cylinder shapes Ms Raskill put on the bench in the art room, but I couldn't do anything right. It wasn't like that at Nurralloo with Miss Hopkins. She thought Dad was a weird old hippy who couldn't draw to save his life. She liked landscapes with gum trees in them that looked like real gum trees.

Pine Hills was different. Ms Raskill knew David Grainger's work. She attended gallery openings.

'Christine Grainger,' she said. 'Well, well. We will be expecting great things of you.' She said that at the first art class and I knew I would never be able to paint in her art room, ever.

I would stand at my easel while she played the class music to create the right creative ambience and I would pick up my leaden paintbrush.

Nothing worked. It was as though the Country Chrissie from Nurralloo whose paintings used to sing with colour was dead. In her place was City Chrissie, sorry – Christine – who killed a painting even before it got from her head to the paper in front of her.

'Oh well, Christine, we can't all inherit the right genes, can we? Conception is a DNA lottery. I'm sure you take after your mother. She must be creative in her own right. What does she do, Christine?'

I wasn't going to tell Ms Raskill that my mother was waitressing at the Queen Victoria Hotel Bistro so I shrugged.

'No need to be sulky, Christine,' she said sharply, 'I mark on attitude, you know. One has to. Can't expect a class of budding Picassos at Pine Hills.'

I didn't feel like painting at home, either. I couldn't walk in from school and go to my room and take out the box of paint tubes Dad had given me for my birthday while he lay on the couch watching the telly, too weak to walk the length of the house to the little sun room Mum had set up as a temporary studio.

I had my Nature Journal. We did Environmental Studies with Mr Chapman. Like my Dad, Mr Chapman was a smoker, so we did a lot of nature walks down to the creek. He would light up, inhale deeply and point to the native grasses that had been planted, the tadpoles just hatched and the mozzie wrigglers they ate. We had to keep a Nature Journal to record our observations and yes, he said, when I asked, of course you can draw in it, Chrissie. This is your book, your observations.

I wanted to tell him about smoking, but I didn't want to tell him about Dad, so I shut up and just moved downwind of his smoke.

I worked so hard on my Nature Journal, Dee said I was meeting boys at the creek.

'Better watch yourself, Chrissie Grainger, you'll go to Hell if you do things at the creek.'

'What things?' I asked.

I still hung around with Dee, not because I wanted to, but because she was there. We were stuck with each other because there was no one else.

'Get off the grass. You know what I mean — kissing. Well, kissing isn't so bad. Letting boys see your knickers. Letting them touch you. That's bad!'

'I'm working on my Nature Journal,' I said, 'I'm not down there with a boy. I don't want to be there with a boy.'

'Then you must be down there smoking.'

'I don't smoke,' I said, shoving my fist in my pocket.

'Show us the journal then.'

She examined the smudged pages carefully, slowly reading my comments aloud.

'Frog spawn! Gross! That's so disgusting!'

'If you smoke,' I said, 'your lungs turn to pulpy sponges and when they squeeze them, black stuff oozes out.'

'You're so weird, Chrissie. I was talking about frogspawn, not smoking. Hey, this one's grouse. I really like this.'

She pointed to a page on which I'd drawn a little Willy Wagtail balancing on a thin twig.

'It's cute.'

'You can have it if you want?' I said.

'Really? Do you really mean it? I'll get Dad to frame it if you let me have it.'

I tore out the page for her and after she had carefully put it between the pages of her maths book, she linked her arm through mine.

'Tell you what, Chrissie, why don't you come to my place this arvo? Mum's taken Matthew to the dentist. Dad'll be home, but he doesn't care what I do.'

'I don't know. I said I'd be straight home.'

'So, you can ring from my place.'

Dee's house was big and although she didn't have a dog or a vegie garden of her own, she had a trampoline in the backyard and a basketball hoop was attached to one side of the double garage.

'Okay,' I said, 'so long as I can have a go on the trampoline.'

'Oh, that's so boring,' Dee said, 'I want to show you my bedroom.'

'I've seen your bedroom, Dee.'

'Only once. We can play some music. I've got a new cassette player.'

'After I have a go on the trampoline.'

It took Dad fifteen rings to answer the phone.

'Hey,' I said, in my bright public voice, 'how are things going?'

'Watching a Rock Hudson movie. Where are you?'

'I'm at Dee's, okay? I'll be home in a little while.'

'Whatever,' Dad said. He sounded tired. 'Walk straight home, okay, baby? And don't talk to strangers.'

Dee was sprawled next to her father, watching a game show.

'Is it cool?' she asked.

'Yeah.'

'Hey Puss,' her dad said as she slid off, 'get us another can before you disappear, right?'

'Don't you reckon my dad's good looking?' she said when we were in her pink and white bedroom, 'he's a bit of a hunk, eh?'

'I suppose. If you like moustaches.'

'I love moustaches,' Dee said opening the top drawer of her white pine dressing table. 'Look, I'll paint your fingernails, for you. I've got this new colour, Miss Pearl'

'I thought I could have a go on the trampoline.'

'Didn't I tell you? It's been put away — Mum thought it might rain.'

'But you promised.'

'I didn't promise, Chrissie. Anyway, I forgot.'

'Can't your dad get it out again for us?'

'But I don't want a go. I told you. It's boring. And anyway, we can't disturb Dad.'

'I don't want my fingernails painted.'

'Well, you can watch me paint mine then,' Dee said, and took out a little velvety bag. She spilled the contents on to the chenille bedspread. There was a pair of tweezers, an orange stick, an emery board, a pair of small gold-handled scissors and a bottle of pearly pink nail polish.

'Mum lets me use her cuticle cream and her nail and hand cream every night, just a drop, to make my fingernails strong. She says chipped nails are a disgrace.'

I sat on my hands. I was a nail biter.

'My mum says nail polish contains chemicals that just dry out your nails! And,' as Dee picked up a lipstick, 'most lipstick contains beef fat.'

'Beef fat? That's disgusting. It does not! You'd be able to taste it. Lipstick doesn't taste like that, it's sort of perfumey.'

'They put that in, to disguise the beef fat.'

Dee dropped the lipstick.

'So what happens when a boy kisses you?'

'I suppose it depends on whether or not you're wearing lipstick.'

Dee looked worried, 'Do you reckon they can taste it?'

'I don't know. Anyway, so what. Who wants to kiss boys?'

'I do. But you don't have to worry about it Chrissie Grainger. Look at you — no boy would want to kiss you looking like that.'

I looked in the mirror. I looked the same as I always did. I was wearing an old soft T-shirt, perhaps a little short, and a pair of denim overalls. They were one of three pairs my mother had got from Toowoomba when we still lived in Nurralloo, and by now you could see my ankle bone, but that looked quite summery. I liked my ankle bones, they were thin and stuck out like a horse's fetlock. The tops of my sandals were peeling because I scuffed them when I walked, even though my mother was always telling me to lift my feet. I had scraped my shoulder length hair into a pony tail that morning and I thought, if anything, it looked a little neater than usual. I leant forward into the mirror. There was probably a new freckle on my nose, but really that was all I could think of that might make me impossible to love.

'What's wrong with the way I look?' I asked.

'Chrissie Grainger, if you can't see what's wrong, there's no point in me trying to tell you. It seems to me that you don't know diddley swat about anything important in this life, even if your father is an artist and you can draw willy wagtails.'

I knew things, I thought, as I trudged slowly home. I knew things Dee couldn't imagine. I knew how to sit quietly for hours at the creek, just watching as all sorts of things lived out their tiny lives. I knew what it was to wake up every morning and hear your father dying little by little, just down the hallway. I knew how it was to hold so much sadness inside yourself that you felt that even a drop more and you'd explode. The sadness would break you open, scatter tiny bits of you right across the floor and the whole you would be gone forever.

'I want some new clothes,' I said to Dad when I got home.

'New clothes, why?' Dad said, looking up from the book he was reading at the table.

'Oh Dad, look at me! Can't you see? My overalls are too short, this top rides up all the time and I need a bra.' I stuck my chest out at him and waited for him to laugh. He looked me up and down and nodded slowly.

'Yes, you're right, Chrissie. You're growing up fast. So, do you have any ideas about these new clothes?'

'Not overalls,' I said quickly, 'we're not in the country now. I want a skirt, a leather skirt. A short leather skirt. And a top with laces and big floppy sleeves. And sandals. Sandals with a little heel.'

'Could we settle for a fake leather mini?' Dad asked, 'after all, we're vegetarians.'

'Sure,' I said, 'I don't think Dee's is real anyway.'

'Okay,' Dad said, 'a fake leather mini, a top, sandals with a heel, a bra — anything else?'

'A training bra,' I said, 'that's what you call it, a training bra.'

'A training bra,' Dad repeated, 'What exactly does that do?'

I wasn't sure, I'd just heard talk of them at school, so I ignored him and continued with my list.

'A pair of jeans,' I said, remembering running with Bongo and the creek. 'Flares.'

'Okay, let's note that flares are desirable according to budget. So we'll make a shopping date, Chrissie.'

'You'll take me?'

'I'll take you,' Daid said, 'I like shopping and your mother doesn't. We might leave that training bra for her, though.'

'I don't want you to get ... I mean, will you manage?'

'I'll enjoy it,' Dad said, 'it's been ages since I've been shopping.'

'I'm going shopping with my Dad,' I told Dee.

'With your Dad?'

'Yes, with my Dad. I'm getting a mini, like yours.'

'You won't get anything like this in Brisbane,' Dee said, smoothing down her skirt and showing off her long pink fingernails. 'My cousin brought this back from America.'

'And I'm getting flares, a new top and sandals with a heel.'

I missed school for the day to go shopping with Dad. He drove carefully, like an old man, but when he got out of the car he was humming just under his breath.

We went straight to David Jones and he made me try everything on and parade in front of him as though I were a model. At first I was embarrassed but he frowned and said, 'Shoulders straight, Chrissie. How can I possibly see what you look like when you're stooped like that? That colour suits you, there — look at that.' And he wheeled me around to face the mirror. 'See how it makes your skin look warm?' He pulled my hair up to the top of my head and turned my chin towards him so I had to squint sideways at my face.

'She's a pretty girl,' the shop assistant said, 'and you are so right about the colour. What a lucky girl, having a dad who can take you shopping. And one who knows about girls' things.'

Dad didn't like any of the skirts. 'Feel them,' he ordered, 'they feel like — what?'

'Plastic,' I said, 'kind of hot and sticky.'

'Revolting,' Dad agreed, 'but the top's good. And it has the right sleeves and here's a denim skirt, much more practical. And here — oh Chrissie, here's a dress for you.'

It was long, with a sort of scooped neck and

the colours were crazy, all jumbled up and dancing across it in pinks, oranges, greens and blues.

'I can't wear that to school,' I said, 'it's too good.'

'Not to school,' Dad said, 'but to my exhibition opening and to lunch with your old man, after we've bought it. Try it on.'

It went right down to my ankles. I could feel it soft against my legs when I walked.

'She'll wear it,' Dad said, 'just cut the tag off.'

'Shall I do her hair? The way you had it, sir? I've a comb here and I'm sure I could find a couple of pins.'

She brought out a comb and tugged it through my hair and when she was through I looked at a ballerina in the mirror, all eyes and bones.

'You'll have to do something about the shoes,' she said looking down at my tatty black sandals, 'they've got some new stock over in shoes. Just the right thing, little heel and a daisy in the front.'

'Thank you,' Dad said, 'thank you for all the trouble you've gone to.' And they smiled at each other as though they shared a secret.

The dress made me hold my shoulders back and the little bubble of hair seemed to pull my head straight and high, so I didn't stumble-kick forward the way I usually walked, scuffing my feet along, chin to my chest.

My new sandals made a satisfying clip-clop

sound crossing the street and I felt very tall. We walked into the dark cave of a restaurant called Captain Cook's Cabin. There was a large aquarium at the front and fishing nets strung from the walls. It was all dark and blue and green, like being underwater. I wasn't sure if Dad was feeling ill or whether the light in the place gave everything a greenish tinge.

He sounded okay as he ordered two half dozen oysters au natural.

'Oysters?' I asked.

'Yes, Chrissie, there's a time in every person's life when they have to eat oysters. Long ago I promised myself I'd introduce you to your first oyster and now is the time.'

They looked like large jellied eyeballs, or the neatly bagged contents of a small stomach. They looked like shelled snails, turned inside out. There were six of them, still in their shells. There were six stomach-churning mouthfuls sitting smugly in front of me, resting on ice, garnished with a sprig of parsley, a lemon wedge and a couple of tiny pieces of brown bread. I opened my mouth to say that there was no way on earth I could possibly swallow something that looked as though it had been retrieved from a surgical operation, when I looked down at my dress, swirling to my ankles.

'Now don't chew them,' Dad said, 'you slide them down your throat, okay?'

He demonstrated, delicately dislodging one

from its shell, squeezing it with lemon and then letting the whole thing disappear into his mouth.

I tried not to see the oyster. I tried to let the colours of my dress fill my mind. I squeezed the lemon, tipped and swallowed. There was the taste of the ocean, a slide of glob down my throat and only five to go.

After the oysters, Dad paid the bill and we left. I was still hungry but I looked at his face and didn't ask for fish and chips. When we left, I let him hold my hand as though I was a little kid again. We walked slowly back to the car and didn't say anything much for the rest of the day.

When Mum came home that evening, I did my catwalk strut for her, modelling my new clothes.

'You shouldn't have done that, Dave,' she said.

'I wanted to,' Dad said in a voice I had never heard before. It was final and almost angry and I looked at him, shocked. Mum didn't say anything more except that yes, the dress was beautiful, very beautiful and I looked very grown up in it.

'We ate oysters,' I said, 'because everyone has to be able to and they were okay. They tasted like the ocean, not half as disgusting as they looked. I ate six whole oysters.'

'And now you're exhausted,' Mum said to Dad and her voice was different too, flat, as though it had been ironed.

'And shall go to bed,' Dad said, getting up

slowly, 'I'm glad we found the dress, Chrissie, and I'm delighted to have taught you about oysters. Stop it, Rhetta love, exhaustion isn't the end of the world.

I wore my new sandals and skirt to school the next day and Dee said, that although my skirt wasn't leather, it was a good length and the cut suited me. She let me read her magazine during lunch.

'Trash,' Ms Raskill said, walking past. 'I'm not surprised at you, Dee, secretarial expectations are all you could aim for, but Chrissie Grainger I expected more from you with your background.'

'She's a Women's Libber,' Dee whispered when Ms Raskill had gone, 'That's why she's a Ms and not plain Miss like everyone else. Some days she doesn't wear a bra. I've seen her, you know, poking out.'

I didn't care about Ms Raskill or her nipples. I didn't even care that I nearly failed Art and had to go to the principal's office with Mr Chapman and listen while she said words like 'sullen' and 'uncooperative' until eventually they asked me to leave the office and I sat outside on the detention bench while they argued about me.

I didn't care because I had a growing list of things I now knew that would be useful in the high-heeled world Dee couldn't wait to join. I knew that sometime in the future I'd be nearly as pretty as my mother. Dad had shown me my future face and even if I couldn't get it to look like that all the time, it had once and would again. He'd promised that. I knew that clothes weren't just about how they looked, but also that you had to be able to touch them, the same way you touched flowers when you walked past particularly lovely ones. And bigger than all of that, I knew that sometimes you had to do the impossible, like eat oysters, or go shopping even when you could hardly breathe, because that's what people did when they truly loved one another, and it had nothing to do with freckles or anklebones or lipstick.

I didn't fail art. Mr Chapman came out and asked me to walk him to his car. He said that my Nature Journal was every bit as important an art document as Ms Raskill's dab and flick paintings, that to call me sullen and uncooperative said more about her than it did about me and that I shouldn't mind these things, but to continue being brave and strong and if there was anything I wanted to talk to him about, I was welcome to do so.

'I don't think you should smoke,' I blurted out loud, watching him as he ferreted around in his pocket for matches, 'I really don't, Mr Chapman. I don't think you should smoke at all.'

He put the matches back in his pocket and tucked the unlit cigarette back in its packet and opened his mouth but I didn't wait to hear what he was going to say.

'I've got to go,' I said desperately, 'I've really got to go. Thank you, Mr Chapman for that stuff, and I'm really sorry.' I took off, my school bag bumping against my legs as I ran.

When I got to school the next day there was a little note on my desk.

Dear Chrissie, it said, *When I was a boy, growing up, we didn't know it was dangerous to smoke. You are quite right, though, now we do know the dangers associated with smoking, it is wrong to continue to do so. I shall try to give up this Christmas holidays. I think Christmas is a good time to try because I am home more and my wife doesn't like me smoking in the house because I make the curtains stink. Thank you for your concern.*
Yours sincerely,
William Chapman.

I folded the note up neatly and put it straight in my school bag before anyone, especially Dee, could see it. As soon as I got home, I put it safely under the flowered paper in my undies drawer. I knew I would keep it for the rest of my life.

Nan and Badger

I rang Nan because no one else seemed about to do it. Dad said it wasn't up to him, it had to be Mum's decision, and Mum refused point blank.

'The last thing I need is her fussing around.'

So every Friday night we rang Nan but we didn't tell her. We talked in false cheery voices about everything except the thing we were all thinking about.

'So, do you like living in the city?' Nan always asked.

'Not much,' I always replied, 'but it's okay.'

'I don't understand why you all moved. I thought you were happy at Nurralloo?'

'I don't know,' I always had to say. Mum stood right next to me when we rang Nan, so close I could almost hear her heart beating. I knew she was ready to grab the phone from me if I said a single wrong thing.

'You make me tell lies,' I said to Mum, 'you make me say things that aren't even true.'

'I can't cope with her on top of everything,' Mum said slowly, the way she did these days when she was angry. 'I have enough to do without looking after my mother as well.'

'You wouldn't have to look after her,' I said, 'she'd help. She'd want to help. You just hate her.'

'I don't hate my mother,' Mum said, 'you're just too young to understand.'

'I hate you,' I said and for a moment I almost believed myself.

Mum sighed and stroked my hair, 'I know,' she said, 'I know.'

I rang Nan one Saturday afternoon when Mum was working at the bistro and Dad was asleep. I sat in the hallway and picked at the scabs on my legs, while I told her the whole story in a queer, little, flat voice I hardly recognised as belonging to me.

'Good God,' she said, 'why on earth didn't your mother tell me?'

I shrugged, but of course she couldn't see me. I couldn't really say anymore. It was as though everything I had said, had used up all my voice.

'You poor little girl,' Nan said, 'you poor little girl.'

It felt like the first time anyone had stopped and looked at me and I started to cry, but silently, the tears leaking through my fingers as I listened to Nan sighing half a dozen loving noises at me and tell me that she was coming up on the fastest plane she could catch, and then I sniffed loudly to let her know I was still alive and hung up.

I knew what I had done was wrong and I didn't care. Nan was all our family. Dad's parents died before I was even born, killed instantly in some horror highway smash, and my other grandfather, Nan's husband, died when Mum was a teenager. His heart gave out. It seemed to me that we were doomed to die young.

'She can't stay here,' Mum said, 'I can't have her here. It's impossible.'

'She'll have to stay somewhere,' Dad said, pouring a cup of lemongrass tea. As he poured it, the air was suddenly sharp with the smell and for a heart-stopping moment I missed Nurralloo, where we'd grown our own lemongrass just beside the back door.

'She can stay in my room,' I said, 'I don't mind.'

Nan arrived with only one small bag. She looked different, too — less grandmotherly than she had two Christmasses ago, the last time I had seen her. She was thinner, sharper. She looked like a television older person. She held Mum closely for a long time and then pushed her away and looked at her face as though searching for something there.

'You should have rung at the very beginning,' she said, 'I know what you're going through. Oh Rhetta, it's so hard, I know. When Keith died I thought my whole life had ended. I know what you must be feeling.'

'Dave's not dead, Mum.'

'No, of course not. Oh sweetheart,' and Nan hugged Mum to her again, but Mum stood still and hard, the way I did sometimes when Mum hugged me when I was angry about something.

'Let's take your bag,' Mum said, 'you'll have to share with Chrissie.'

'That'll be great, won't it Chrissie. You don't mind, do you darling?'

I didn't mind at all even though I had to sleep on a mattress on the floor. It was comfortable because I would wake up in the night and hear Nan snoring her faint, wet, snuffly snores. In the morning she'd get up with me and do the things Mum used to do, make my breakfast, make Dad a cup of tea and cut me sandwiches for lunch all while she talked, almost as though she was talking to herself, but out loud.

'I knew,' she said, 'I knew when Keith died — it came to me like a blow that this was all we had, this one puny life and we'd better make the most of it. But raising a child by yourself, worrying about decisions — I lost it again.'

'What did you lose, Nan?'

She sat down at the kitchen table. Dad was watching her, drinking his tea slowly.

'The knowledge of life,' she said, and when she smiled directly at Dad, she looked so like Mum I nearly dropped my toast.

'I don't understand,' I said, hearing my voice whine upwards.

'You have to be true to yourself,' Dad said, nodding.

'Boldly,' Nan said, 'without worrying what other people might think or how they'll judge you. Like you and Rhetta, Dave. You've always grasped your dreams.'

'That's what you hated about me,' Dad said, 'you wanted Rhetta to marry some up and coming accountant.'

Nan nodded, 'Of course I did. I was wrong, though, wasn't I? You've made her very happy.'

'Thank you,' Dad raised his mug of tea at her, 'I have tried. I am sorry its ending like this.'

'So am I, for both of you.'

When Dad and Nan talked like that together, I hated it. It was as though between them they were inviting death into our house. They discussed it so calmly, at the kitchen table of all places, where you sat eating toast and honey. Mum didn't like it, either.

'You've changed,' she said one day, before she hurried off to work. 'Look at you, sitting there on your second pot of tea and the washing-up's not even done yet.'

'I'm learning that washing-up isn't that important,' Nan said, 'why don't you take the day off, Rhetta? Do you have to rush off like this?'

'Yes! Yes I do! Of course I do! Stupid question!' and Mum stalked off muttering.

Sometimes it seemed as though she was just plain angry at Nan spending time with Dad.

'What do you talk about?' she'd ask Dad, 'what do you both talk about?'

'Just stuff, Rhetta, just stuff. Sometimes money stuff, sometimes the past. Sometimes we look at my art. She wants a coffin too, but she wants to paint it herself. She's going to get Bodhi to measure her up.'

'Oh God,' Mum said, 'it's like a different world here. At work they're all worried about — I don't know, pimples, half of them, and boyfriends and whether or not they are or want to be, pregnant, and who got engaged. And I come here and it's all coffins.'

'You don't have to work, Rhetta, she said she's going to sell the house.'

'I do have to work,' Mum said, 'of course I have to work. I couldn't cope if I didn't work.'

Nan joined a yoga class and started Italian lessons. Some afternoons when I got home from school she'd be doing exercises in the lounge room or she and Dad would be sitting sort of together, sort of apart with their eyes closed and all you could hear was their breathing, Nan's steady and regular, Dad's all ragged and noisy.

'What are you doing? Can I have some cake? I'm starving.'

'Meditating,' Dad said, 'that's what we're doing. Sitting quietly listening to nothing. Count-

ing our breaths. Stilling the chattering monkeys.'

'What monkeys? Can I have two pieces?'

'One only, don't want to spoil your dinner.'
Nan stood up, 'The monkeys inside our heads,
Chrissie, the ones that chatter on about all life's
trivia. We want to be still enough so we disappear into our own hearts.'

'Where's Mum?' my mother said, come home
from the afternoon shift. 'I thought she was
supposed to be here, helping? How can she help
if she's never home?'

'She cooked dinner,' I said. 'Look — lasagne.'

'Where did she go, Dave?'

'I don't know,' Dad said, 'yoga or Italian probably. Or maybe to the movies with that old bloke
she's met?'

'What bloke? Why doesn't she talk to me? Why
doesn't she tell me what's going on?'

'You're not home, Mum,' I said, setting the
table. 'How can she tell you anything when
you're not here?'

'Thanks, Chrissie, thanks a lot. That makes
me feel very good, I don't think. I have to work
you know. I have to work.'

'You don't,' Dad said softly reaching out to her,
'you don't have to work, Rhetta. Your mother's
offered us money.

'You don't understand do you,' and Mum
jumped up from the table. When she came back
later she'd washed her waitressing make-up

from her face and her hair hung loosely around her face.

'I'm just not used to a mother who goes to yoga and speaks in Italian.'

It was true Nan was starting to talk in little bits of Italian. She had a cassette tape she played. She had to answer the voices on the tape. It sounded like rain. The words lilted away from me, I could hear them but I didn't know what they meant and I was always a little bit disappointed when Nan explained that she'd just asked where the nearest supermarket or railway station was.

'Not to mention, goes out with a bloke,' Dad said, watching Mum.

'I'll have to talk to her,' Mum said.

'That would be a really good idea, Rhetta. That might make things a lot easier for both of you.'

'About the bloke,' Mum said, 'that's all, Dave, just about this bloke.'

'Have you changed, Nan?' I asked when she got home late that night.

'Good heavens, Chrissie, I thought you'd be sound asleep. What do you mean have I changed? I've still got my good trousers on.'

'No, other stuff. Like inside.'

She didn't talk for a while. The room was filled with other night-time noises, her zipper being pulled down, the rustling sound of her shirt, Dad coughing down the hallway and Bongo dreaming of rabbits.

'Yes,' she said finally, 'yes, I think I have changed. I should have done all this years ago. It's too easy to get caught up in the stupid little things of life, to make them all that matters. It shouldn't take death to make us see that, but often it does. Do you know, Chrissie, when I first met your mum's father, we'd drive off in his car, he had an MG then, very smart, and we'd drive down to Watson's Bay or Coogee. We'd sit for hours watching the waves. Sometimes we'd kiss, but a lot of the time we'd talk, planning our life. We were going to have five children, three boys and two girls. We were going to build a big house somewhere and I was going to have a garden full of roses out the front, vegies out the back. I was going to have chooks, too. I loved chooks. He was going to drive off every day and come home every evening when the children would be all rosy from their baths. We'd sit in the evening and read, or listen to the radio.'

'But you only had Mum. You didn't have five kids.'

'No, that's right. In the end I could only have one child. We didn't need a big house after all. Keith drove off every day, and came home as he promised and there were his girls, that's what he called your mother and me, and Rhetta would be all rosy from her bath, but we didn't sit together in the evening because there was always some work to do. And then Rhetta went to school and I did this and that. She grew into a

leggy girl with a mind of her own, always shouting at me. And then Keith keeled over, just
crumpled up one day.'

'Oh Nan,'

'Don't cry, Chrissie, that's not the point. The
point is that once upon a time, I was a dreamer
and somewhere along the way I forgot how to be.
Your father's helped me find that girl again.'

'Is it true that you've *met* someone?'

Nan laughed and bent right down to my mattress and slipped her arms around me, lifting
me into a hug, 'I've met a lot of people,' she said,
'I've met my yoga teacher, I've met my Italian
teacher. Do you know, I've talked to more people
this past month than I do all year round in
Sydney?'

'That's not what I meant.' I could smell her
perfume. It wasn't the powdery scent that clung
to her during the day, but a deeper smell, with
roses.

'Yes. Yes, I have met someone.'

'Is that why you've bought jeans? Mum said
she's never seen you in jeans ever in her entire
life. Dad said that was a shame, because they
looked good on you.'

'That was nice of your dad and no, I didn't buy
jeans because of Badger, I bought them because
I've never worn them and I wanted to, just to see
if I liked wearing them.'

'Is Badger the bloke? And do you like wearing
them?' I was feeling sleepy now. I'd felt sleepy

the moment Nan had put her arms around me, as though her perfume was a spell, a sleeping spell winding into my brain.

'Yes, Badger's the bloke, and yes, I like jeans. Good night, Chrissie, good night.'

Badger came round after that, for dinner. Nan fussed in the kitchen with all Mum's cook books spread across the table. She wasn't used to it, she said. In the old days she would have just cooked a good plain roast but now we were all vegetarians, it was difficult. Mum got home and instead of heading straight for the shower and spending hours in there, washing the grease out of her hair, she put on her apron and made soothing noises at Nan as they both mixed and stirred. They made ravioli, just like they did in Italy, Nan said, and the kitchen smelled peaceful and warm. It reminded me of Nurralloo, when Mum would let me help her cook, but I didn't really want to help this time. I just wanted to sit watching Mum and Nan.

Badger arrived with bottles of wine, flowers for Nan and Mum and some tiny, brightly coloured fruit, nestled like little ornaments in a box like a chocolate box.

'What is it?' I asked.

'Marzipan fruit,' he said.

'It looks so real,' I said sticking out my finger and delicately nudging a miniature apple, 'what's marzipan?'

'Almonds,' Nan replied, 'and sugar. What a treat, Badger.'

Badger looked pleased. He was a tall old man, older even than Nan. His hair was dark grey and stood up like a brush all over the top of his head. On either side of his mouth were deep lines that looked as though they'd swallow his smile, but when he did smile, they just vanished into the other, smaller creases on his face and his pale grey eyes seemed to darken all of sudden and I felt I had to smile back, quickly in case he turned away from me before he could see that I was glad he was there.

'Why is he called Badger,' I asked Nan later, 'it's weird.'

'He's a bit like a badger, I suppose,' Nan said. She was doing her yoga in the lounge room. 'Look at this, Chrissie, remember how stiff I was when I first started?'

'What do you mean, like a badger?'

'You've read *The Wind in the Willows*?'

'When I was little,' I said, 'and anyway, that's just a story.'

'Well, badgers are private, shy creatures. They're interesting, intriguing and very attractively striped.'

'Badger hasn't got stripes.'

'No,' Nan said, and smiled, 'but he is very attractive.'

'Nan's in love,' I told my mother when she

came home from the afternoon shift, 'she's in love with Badger.'

'Don't be ridiculous,' Mum said, 'they're friends, that's all.'

'She said he was very attractive and she smiled in that way.'

'What way?'

'The way people smile when they're thinking about kissing.'

'Oh, Chrissie, you do make things up, you silly girl.'

'It's true,' Dad said, coming up behind her and kissing her neck. 'They're in love. Isn't that great? Fancy walking into a senior's yoga class and meeting someone who makes you smile because you can't help thinking about kissing them. It's a beautiful thing, Rhetta.'

'It's disgusting,' Mum said, and she spent a long time in the shower and when she came out she was all shiny, as though she had been polished.

'Why is it disgusting?' I asked Dad, 'Why does Mum think its disgusting, Nan and Badger?'

'Your mother's sad,' Dad said, 'and when you're sad, everything's hard, even kissing.'

'Are you sad?' As soon as I said it I could have bitten off my own tongue, but the words were out, hanging still in the air, like a sky message.

'Of course I am,' Dad said, stroking my hair, 'I'm sad about leaving you all behind. Some days I feel so sad I can't bear it. But it's easier for me because I'm the one going on. Each day my body gives up a little more, so it becomes a little closer and I can feel another little piece of this life slipping off me, slipping away. My body is teaching me how to leave. You don't have to understand that, Chrissie, but remember it, remember that while my heart is sad, it's also being slowly taught to say goodbye. And I'm very pleased Nan's here, too. You did the right thing. You're a brave girl and that makes me feel good, knowing how brave you are. You really are your mother's daughter.'

'I don't want to hear any more,' I said.

We had conversations like that, my father and I, and Nan and I. We had an agreement that when I wanted to, I could stop them talking. When it got too much I could go to my room. Or I could walk right out of the house, with Bongo and we'd go down to the river and muck about until we both smelled of river mud and were so dirty we'd have to hose off out the back before we were allowed in the house.

'You would never have let me get that dirty,' Mum said when she came home to find Nan hosing me.

'No,' Nan agreed, 'how stupid of me, Rhetta. I wanted you to be perfect, to show the world what a good mother I was. I am sorry. I felt if I could keep you clean and neat, you'd be safe. I didn't know what else to do, how else to protect you.'

'And you would never have hosed me down

outside. You'd have smacked me hard, then you would have dragged me into the laundry and you'd have scrubbed until every inch of me was rubbed red. You were a terrible, terrible mother. You hated small children. You hated the mess I made. Why are you so goddamn wonderful now? Why do you have to be such a perfect mother to her, when you were never, never good to me?'

The hose dropped and Nan went over to my mother and held her. I stood there dripping but they didn't care. Mum was still shouting but the words were all muffled because she was shouting into Nan's shoulder, and I couldn't hear and I didn't want to hear.

'Were you a terrible mother?' I asked Nan that night, 'Did you really hate small children?'

'I loved my house,' Nan said, 'It didn't matter that it wasn't the one we were going to build, Keith and I. I loved it because it was ours and it was perfect. And that's how people judged you then — you were a good wife and mother if your children were clean and neat and your house was pretty and spotless. And you had to be able to make a good sponge.'

'I wasn't a natural housekeeper,' Nan said, leaning back into her pillows. 'I didn't like having to do the same thing over and over and have nothing to show for it but an absence; an absence of dirt, an absence of mess. I had to force myself to do the floors every day and to dust every day and to tidy every day, and so, yes, I don't think I was any fun as a mother.'

'Mum was fun,' I said, 'in Nurralloo. We used to cook together, you know? She didn't seem to mind how much flour went on the floor. Dad sketched us at the table.'

'I'm sure Rhetta is a much, much, better mother than I was,'

'She's changed, and you've changed, and its gone topsy-turvy,' I said, squirming round to look at Nan, 'Mum's gone so hard, she snaps like a really fresh gingernut biscuit and you've gone soft.'

'Apart from my thigh and calf muscles,' Nan said laughing. 'Don't worry, Chrissie, your mother will stop snapping. She's got a lot on her plate, more than anyone should have.'

'She needn't,' I said, 'Dad said she doesn't have to work that hard.'

'Maybe she does have to, just for a while, for herself. You don't always work for the money. I wish I'd been able to work after Keith died. You know, when your mother went to school, I used to just go back to bed. I used to go back to bed and try to sleep for as long as I could, just so I wouldn't have to feel so alone.'

'Why didn't you get a job?'

Nan shrugged, 'I didn't know what to do.'

'So did you sleep all the time?'

'That's what it felt like. A whole year, maybe two, of sleep. Like Snow White.'

'And Badger's woken you up?' I snorted, thinking of Badger leaning over Nan, kissing her awake.

'I think I've been slowly waking up, inch by inch, over the years. And this, not just Badger, but this whole thing — Dave, yoga, your mother and you, Chrissie, have been the final wake-up nudges.'

'Will Mum sleep when, I mean if ...'

'No, she won't sleep. She has to stay awake for you, Chrissie, and that's why she's working so hard now.'

I didn't understand everything. It didn't seem likely that Nan really slept for that long but I also knew just how tired you could get being sad. Sadness rested over our house the way I had seen clouds sit on top of mountains, and some days we seemed to move slowly through it, as though the cloud had turned into leaden fog and each movement we made required just a little more effort than we could bear to make. Only Nan seemed to step through these times lightly. Maybe it was the yoga, I thought, strengthening her legs or maybe it was because she had done all that sleeping those years ago when Mum was a shouting teenager.

One night Nan came home with Badger and they both looked smiley and secret. He whispered to her, in the hallway outside our room, 'Do you want me to stick around?'

'No, better not,' she said, 'it wouldn't be right, you getting caught up in any flak.'

When he'd gone. Nan announced that she was moving out of our house and into Badger's.

'I don't believe you're doing this,' Mum said, 'I don't believe a woman of your age would do such a stupid thing.'

'You can't move,' I said, 'Nan, you can't move.'

'I hate going, Dave,' she said to my father, 'I know it just seems like the wrong time but I don't think it is. I think you and Rhetta need to be together and I know Badger and I do. I won't be far away. It's just that I won't be living here full-time.'

'Why do you have to go?' Mum demanded. 'Just why? Tell me one good reason, and I don't mean that nonsense about Dave and me needing time. We need you. Chrissie needs you. We need you here.'

Mum slammed into her bedroom. We could hear her banging things on her dressing table. Then she came out waving her hairbrush around.

'What right have you got to be happy,' she shouted. 'What right have you got to be making plans!'

And she threw her hairbrush down. It bounced and landed at Nan's feet.

'You know I would give you anything,' Nan said, 'anything at all. If I could I'd take my own lungs out, but I can't, I can't.' She walked up to my mother and then she took off the long string of amber she always wore and put it around my mother's neck. I don't think Mum even noticed because she was crying too hard and her hands were over her eyes.

We did see Nan all the time. She dropped in nearly every day and we went over to her place too, and it was almost as if she hadn't left except Mum wore the amber necklace all the time and seemed to soften a little as though it wasn't only the hairbrush that had cracked that afternoon but also a casing she'd made around herself. Although she still worked at the bistro, because she said it kept her sane, she stopped working back-to-back shifts and weekends and was at home more often. Sometimes when I got home from school she'd be lying with Dad on the couch, not talking or watching television, just lying close and for a minute or two I'd forget everything and just be happy to see them like that.

Nan bought Mum a new hairbrush, made of boar's bristle with a wooden handle. It was the kind of hairbrush, Nan said, that would last you a lifetime, if you didn't lose it somewhere. They were made in England and you could only buy them at David Jones. Mum had her hair cut because of the grease smell and the washing but she used Nan's brush every night, first on me counting one hundred strokes and then on herself, when she'd take the amber necklace off and hang it around my neck so the brush wouldn't get caught in it and pull it and maybe break it. I'd stand there counting the honey-coloured beads as my mother counted brush-strokes. I knew the amber was special because my grandfather, not Badger, had given Nan the necklace when they got engaged. He'd brought it back from the War. Amber was for eternity, Nan said, but she also pointed out the little lives that had been trapped in it, insect parts and fly wings, so I was never sure whether eternity was a good thing or not.

Leprosy, Leonardo and Father Damien

I knew these facts off by heart: Father Damien arrived in the leper's colony of Kalaupapa in 1873, later he himself contracted leprosy and he died in 1889. I knew that leprosy often begins as a small dot in the palm of one's hand. You shouldn't call it leprosy, Mr Chapman said, it was really Hansen's Disease and the fact that it was still called leprosy in our textbooks went to show you how behind Queensland was in the education system.

I had a small red dot on my palm. I couldn't remember it being there when we lived in Nurralloo. It wasn't a freckle or a mole, it was a definite dot. It looked a little as though someone had jabbed with a red ballpoint pen or the sharp end of a compass, not hard enough for blood to bead on the surface, just hard enough for it to leak under my skin and form a pin prick red dot.

At night I would wake screaming from dreams

in which my fingers or my nose slowly crumbled. I wouldn't even know it was happening and then in the dream I'd look down, casually, see myself in a mirror, and I'd realise in horror why the people in the street or the supermarket had backed away from me. Dad would come in when I screamed and hold me and rock me. He always asked what I had dreamt about but I never told him. It wasn't fair to tell him about the leprosy dreams when his lungs were covered with real hot spots, cancerous cells that might be still multiplying themselves.

I hated the chapter on Father Damien but I couldn't stop reading it, over and over again. Leprosy starts with a tingling and then a numbness in the extremities, often the digits. Your fingers begin to rot. The book said that when Father Damien took confession, sometimes he had to hold his nose for the stench of rotting flesh. At first he slept out in the open, rather than share a hut with a leper, and he ate his food from a flat rock. I couldn't understand how he could bear to eat. Fingers and toes fall off, noses crumble back into the face of the victim, and eventually, before you die, your whole body becomes numb to pain.

There had been cases of leprosy in Australia, up north. There had been a leper's colony in Queensland. There were still leper colonies in India. One of the problems with leprosy is that you feel no pain in your hardened skin, so you can burn yourself hideously and not know. I stuck pins in the thickened skin around my red dot, stuck them in harder and harder until I bled, just to make sure I could feel the sharp point going in. Some days I seemed to have to jab harder than other days. Some days I could hardly feel a thing.

My mother's hands were rough from washing the glasses at the bistro. You washed them with a little methylated spirits in the water so the glasses shone. She seemed to often burn herself, pulling things out from our oven. I asked her if a particularly ugly burn hurt and she said, 'No, I hardly felt it when it happened and it still doesn't hurt. Looks horrible though,' and we both stared at the welt near her thumb.

It was hard to tell if my original spot had grown larger, or whether the pin pricks made it seem larger. Sometimes I got a tingly feeling in my fingers, a little like pins and needles. It happened most often in the morning, when I woke up and it was usually in the left hand, the hand I tucked under my head when I went to sleep. I wondered if I should write my symptoms down, the way Dad was keeping a pain journal.

I was really scared when my left hand ring finger went numb after the Friday sports afternoon. I went home and peered at my palm through the old magnifying glass I used to start small fires sometimes. The whirly lines on my skin looked huge and the dot was definitely not a freckle. It was not a little pimple, like the kind my mother called sweat pimples. It was not a mole. It wasn't a scar. I could think of only one thing it could be ...

It takes ages to die of leprosy. That is one of the horrible things about it, gradually all of you thickens, and goes numb, the way my finger was. I was sad about that finger.

Mum sometimes wore turquoise and lapis lazuli rings from India and I had tried one on and worn it for a whole weekend.

It wasn't possible that the rings, even though they came from India, could carry leprosy germs. And I hadn't worn it on my ring finger anyway, but on my thumb.

I found one of my mother's old cotton gloves that she'd worn back when she'd tried to look after her hands. The idea was that you smeared moisturiser over your hands and then slept with the gloves on and when you woke up your hands were softer than a baby's bottom. It was too hot, though to sleep with your hands in gloves, Mum said and anyway, what with the washing up at the bistro, hardly worth it.

I didn't think it was too hot. I put the left hand glove on and then I couldn't see the hardening skin and the give-away red dot and no one else could, either.

'Allergies,' I told Mr Chapman at school and he didn't question me any further.

'Allergies,' I told everyone in class, 'I have this

cream, see, and the glove helps it soak in. I have to wear it even in bed.'

'Growing your fingernails' Dad asked at breakfast, 'or is this a new fashion?'

Mum was on morning shift at the bistro. While we were eating our Wheat Bix, she had been working already for three hours, serving bacon and eggs easy side over to the American business men who tipped so well .

'Oh, you know,' I said, tucking my gloved hand under the table, 'just a school thing.'

We had to write an essay called 'Your Hero' for Mr Chapman. I chose Father Damien. I said he was my hero because he had worked with the lepers even though he knew he would eventually get leprosy and die. I said he was my hero because he had died young and had kept working right up until his death. I wrote the essay with my gloved hand in my lap. I traced the picture of Father Damien from our history book and put it up in the top left hand corner of the paper. It was a picture from before he had leprosy. He wasn't particularly handsome, his mouth was too big and he wore daggy glasses and clutched a crucifix in his hands.

I wondered if it was really heroic to die when you didn't have to. Was my father not heroic, because he didn't have a choice about dying? Would he be more heroic if, instead of making art, he'd taken us all to live in Africa, where people starved every day? Would I be considered a hero, dying so young and terribly of the leprosy which must be slowly, very slowly, spreading from my left palm to the tips of my fingers?

The more I thought about Father Damien, the more I began to dislike him. What made him think the lepers wanted to hear about God, anyway? If your fingertips had crumbled away and your nose had caved in, would you be that interested in praying? Would Dee still go to church if her father was dying? Why did you have to *want* to die before you were a hero?

I didn't take off my glove at all, even to wash my hand. It didn't get dirty, so what was the point? Anyway, I didn't want water on it, that might speed up the rotting process. I didn't prod it anymore, either. I knew what was going on under the white, ladylike glove and it was terrible.

I handed my essay on Father Damien in to Mr Chapman. I had included detailed descriptions of how at first he had slept in the open air to avoid the smell of decaying flesh but then he'd overcome his revulsion and even eaten with the lepers, eaten out of the same bowl with his bare fingers. And how he had washed the lepers' sores, heedless of his own health.

Most of the other kids did sporting heroes or movie stars. One kid even did their grand-dad, he'd been a soldier. Mr Chapman said my essay showed originality but he hoped next time I would choose a less morbid subject. He said,

'Are you sure that's just an allergy you have? You've been wearing that glove for an awfully long time, Chrissie'.

'Washing up liquid,' I said, 'and even soap, really.'

When I got home from school, Dad was sitting at the kitchen table.

'Put the kettle on, Chrissie,' he said, 'and come and have a biscuit.'

He'd put out some Iced Vo Vo's and I scraped the pink off with my front teeth.

'So how was school?' Dad asked, sitting down next to me.

'Okay.'

'What did you do?'

I couldn't think of anything we'd done that would interest him. 'Nothing much.'

'You must have done something,' he said.

'You know, stuff.' He was sitting on my left hand side and every so often he seemed to look at my gloved hand. I hugged it between my knees and ate another biscuit quickly.

'Chrissie,' Dad said, 'you would tell me if there was anything wrong, wouldn't you?'

I stared at him, 'Wrong? What do you mean?' Hadn't he forgotten something even asking me that?

'I meant at school,' he said. 'You'd tell me if there was something wrong at school.'

'There's nothing wrong at school,' I said, 'nothing at all.'

We sat quietly for a minute. The kitchen door was open and a breeze riffled through. Dad shivered but I turned my hot face towards it with relief.

'I want to see your hand,' Dad said suddenly, 'come on Chrissie, take the glove off.'

'What?'

'The glove, Chrissie, the glove comes off.'

'No,' I hugged my knees tighter together, 'No, I can't.'

Dad grabbed my wrist and pulled. I grabbed the bottom of the kitchen chair with my hand and clung on but the glove slipped on the metal and vinyl and I could see, from Dad's face, that the effort was hurting him so I let him yank my poor dead hand. He peeled the glove off and we both looked down at my hand as though it was a small, sick animal.

It was just a hand. A pale hand with longer fingernails than its mate but no less perfect. The unblemished skin went right up the fingers and swept down the palm side in the whirls and patterns that made my fingerprints unique in the world. The compass prick marks had gone and so had the little red dot. I pinched the skin where my palm left off and my wrist began.

'Ouch,'

'What did you do that for,' Dad asked.

'Just checking'

'Nice fingernails,' Dad said, taking my hand

and examining it, 'they certainly have grown under that glove.'

He turned my hand over, palm side up and before I could stop him, he kissed me right where the spot had been.

'Dad!' I said, snatching my hand away.

'What?'

'You might still get it you know,'

'Get what Chrissie? Girl germs?'

'Leprosy,' I said, sitting on both my hands.

'Leprosy,' Dad said and then he leant back in his chair and laughed and laughed until he started to cough.

'Oh Chrissie,' he said, after I had made him sip a glass of water slowly, 'my darling girl.'

'Father Damien got it and there were cases in Queensland at the turn of the century. They still have it in India. People die of it, I don't think that's funny.'

'I'm sorry,' Dad said, 'but what made you think you had leprosy?'

'There was this spot,' I said, 'honest, and that's how it starts. And then my fingers went numb. And I had these nightmares that my nose had disappeared. It just made sense, okay?'

Dad picked up the glove and threw it in the bin.

'I don't think we need that anymore,' he said.

I threw out my Father Damien project too, although I didn't bother telling Dad.

'Who is a hero of yours,' I asked him later that

evening. He was reading on the couch but he propped the book up on his chest to answer me.

'Let's see — Leonardo da Vinci, I'd say. Yes, Leonardo.'

'Why?'

'He was endlessly curious about the world. And not a bad artist either,' Dad said. 'He kept a notebook, a bit like your Nature study book, full of drawings of the way things worked, like the motion of waves, cloud formations, flowers — you name it, he stopped and looked at it, recorded it, wondered about it. He's my hero. There's a book of his drawings on my shelf, if you want to have a look.'

I left a note on Mr Chapman's table the next day. I wanted to clear up any confusion.

Dear Mr Chapman, I wrote, *I just want you to know that Father Damien is no longer my hero. I think dying on purpose is a waste. If I were a leper, I'd want someone to be finding a cure, like they should find a cure for cancer, not just pray for me. Leonardo da Vinci is really my hero. He would have found a cure, if he'd been born a bit later.*
Yours sincerely,
Chrissie Grainger

Mr Chapman passed me a note in return, at Little Lunch.

Dear Chrissie,
I think you have made an intelligent choice with Leonardo. Did you know he nearly invented the

*aeroplane? If you need to talk to me about anything
at all, you know you always can.*
Yours sincerely
William Chapman.

He came up to me in the playground and
repeated his offer. I told him, thank you, that
things were okay, really. I was swinging from the
monkey bars, which I hadn't been able to do
because of the slippery glove, and he watched
as I swung across to the other side.

'Allergy better then?' he asked.

'Turned out not to be one,' I said, 'just one of
those mysterious things that go away after a
while.'

'That's good,' he said, 'inconvenient wearing a
glove all the time.'

Not as inconvenient as having leprosy, I
wanted to tell him, but didn't say that either. I
swung up on to the bars again and right across
and back and across until the bell rang. My
arms ached and my hands smelled metallic and
rusty but I knew that by lunch time my arms
would have forgotten the weight of my body and
the desperate lurch from one bar to the next and
I'd want to do it again, just because I could.

Unfinished Business

Nan said that sometimes people stay alive for ages longer than the doctors predict because there is still something they need to do, some unfinished business. Sometimes, she said, this was seeing someone they needed to say goodbye to, sometimes it was an event, like the birth of a child, or a marriage, which kept them living when, according to medical prognosis, they should have been dead. Nan reckoned that Dad's exhibition was keeping him going.

Mr Gable had come around with two of his helpers, minions, he called them and it sounded quite rude. He was Dad's art dealer, a large moist man who wore flowered braces to hold up his large trousers. No one called him Mr Gable. Even his minions just called him Gable as though that was enough.

'Gable,' Dad said, 'back from the States, eh?'

'Dave, I heard the news. I came as soon as I could.'

Gable put his arms around my father, dwarfing him in a bear hug. When he finally released Dad, Gable pulled a handkerchief out of his pocket and blew his nose and wiped his eyes. 'We'll put on a show,' he said, 'up all the prices so you can make some money out of the bastards.'

'You'll make the money.'

'Not me, no Dave, forget it. Just the framing costs.'

'Gable!' Now it was Dad's turn to fossick around for a hanky.

Nan and I took Gable out to the shed and showed him the coffins.

'Dear God,' he said, 'they are beautiful. Dave's sure he wants to go in his?'

'Yes,' I said, 'that's what it's for. That's what he did it for.'

'To face death,' Nan said. 'To be ready for it!'

Gable dusted an old crate and sat down, pulling up his pant legs first, so they wouldn't crease. 'Is it that close?' he asked.

Nan pulled up a second crate. I leant against the table tennis table. I knew all this off by heart. My vocabulary had increased. I knew words like secondaries and metastasise. I knew the names of bits of the body which had never figured in our human body lessons at school; the lymph glands and the pancreas. Most of all, I knew about lungs.

'They've stopped chemo,' Nan said, 'there's no point. He's started morphine. He wants to die at home, not in hospital. Marijuana helps, to a degree. It stops the nausea, promotes appetite. Sources tell me other drug therapies may be more effective.'

Gable looked at me sharply and tipped his head towards me.

'I am allowed to hear anything I want to hear,' I said, 'it's the agreement.'

'Very unorthodox, very Dave,' he muttered, 'I take it,' he said to Nan, 'if I understand correctly, you're talking about heroin?'

Nan nodded, 'There's a rumour it's very effective.'

'Well anything can be obtained,' Gable said frowning, 'but it's costly.'

'Money,' Nan waved, 'that's in hand. I've sold my house. Badger and I get along quite well in his flat. And when this is all over, we're going to India to meet a yoga master.'

'Badger?'

'Badger is her lover,' I said crossly. Lover was a word I had recently learned. It sounded more dignified than boyfriend and less permanent than husband. I hated all this talk about heroin. We'd heard about it at school. There was a book, the diary of a young girl who became hooked and couldn't get off. We all took turns reading it. You could get sick from withdrawing. You sweated and itched and your teeth fell out. Then there was the other problem that it was illegal and we could all be put in jail. And you had to inject it, sometimes in your eyeball because you couldn't find the veins in your arm.

'Ah,' Gable stood up, 'of course. Well, you must let me know if there's anything at all I can do, short of drug dealing.'

'Thank you,' Nan said, 'we'll keep you informed.'

'I um, wouldn't say anything at school about this,' Gable said to me.

'I don't,' I told him, picking my cuticles, 'it's in the agreement.'

'Of course. Of course.'

There were too many things not to say at school. Drugs was only one of them. I didn't say the cancer word at all. I didn't say secondaries or mestastsise or pancreas. I didn't say pain. I didn't say dying. I didn't talk about the euthanasia debate that was currently a nightly show at home. I didn't say that my mother went to work every day because, she told me, it gave her a normal perspective on life and that's why I should go to school, too. Just to learn that everyone in the world wasn't dying. Just to learn that everyone in the world was thinking and talking about stuff other than pain management, legal and otherwise, death and when to die, legal or otherwise.

Dad's theory, which he ran past Bodhi, now a regular visitor, was that he'd simply overdose himself.

'I've never tried smack,' Bodhi said, 'too

scared, man, but I reckon I would, in your position Dave.'

'I just want to get the show out of the way,' Dad said, 'I don't want anything to happen to stuff it up. Gable's terms for the show are very generous. If enough sells Rhetta won't have to work anymore in that stupid job.'

'I don't have to now,' Mum said, 'I want to, Dave. I actually find I quite like it. It's about giving people value for money. You see,' she said turning to Bodhi, 'the Queen Victoria is a top international hotel. The bistro does room service, breakfasts. We get all sorts of visitors. There are glimpses of the world. It was snowing yesterday in Missouri. Can you beat that? It was snowing and this guy, a business man, had just rung his family and the ranch, he actually owns a ranch, was snowed in.'

'Wow,' Bodhi fanned himself, 'that's something isn't it?'

'I wish we'd been able to travel, Rhetta,' Dad said, 'I wanted to take you to Paris.'

They held hands on top of the dining table.

That was what talk did these days — circled around and through hopes and dreams and death. One minute it seemed just as though we were in a television debate, coolly arguing the pros and cons of getting involved in hard drugs for pain relief. Why was the medical profession so cowardly? Why was the government a pack of no-hopers who promoted sleazy drug dealing in back alleys with nameless Mr Bigs laundering their money while in school yards toothless dealers conned kids into having their first hit? I loved the idea of someone washing their money. I thought of taking garbage bags of it to the laundromat, the way we had to when the washing machine broke down. All those dollar bills emerging clean and crisp from the dryer. Then just as I had got over that image, the conversation would shift and we'd be in Dad and Mum's private space of regret and goodbye and we'd have to work out whether or not to leave the room, go and make another cup of tea or put a record on or just go on talking as though they could do that in public and we were cool about it.

Nan was cool about it, often. She'd sometimes get up and put her arms around both of them and just stand there. Bodhi claimed he could sometimes see her aura. It was all purply and blue, he said, which indicated she was a higher being.

'Not me,' Nan said, 'I have done everything too late. I'll need a few more lives to get it right.'

I learnt to try to look at my parents as though they were actors on television. If I pretended I didn't really know them, that this was a drama I was just watching, I could get through their private moments without crying.

Mum said I was growing up too fast. She said I should be in Girl Guides or learning ballet or going horse riding instead of always shadowing their talk, instead of always being involved. She said there was something to be said for the normal nuclear family where no one talked about anything and nothing was said. She said I'd regret all this later, expensively, to some shrink.

Nan said I was growing up at my own rate and that was dictated by all sorts of things, not only external events but internal consciousness. She said the cycles of life and death are muddled over in the West post-industrial capitalist society. She said in an age when babies were plucked from the womb so that an obstetrician could go to golf, what could we expect but a sanitised death?

Mum said I hadn't been plucked from her womb. She had me at home with only natural muscle relaxants and that she was equally prepared for Dave to die at home, too, if it came to that. Dad said he wasn't doing anything for the moment, just putting one foot in front of the other, just getting by one day at a time, thank you.

I knew he was waiting for the exhibition and I was scared. The exhibition would happen. Gable had printed all the invitations. He had unearthed old prints of Dad's from his gallery storeroom and our shed. He brought round stuff for Dave to date and sign. He looked at the work Dad had done since his diagnosis — how many months ago? The new stuff was black and white, like x-rays. It was full of shadows, just like Dad said his lungs were. He was mapping the disease's progress, he said, in his own way. Only the two coffins gleamed, coloured and beautiful, the luminous surface begging your fingers to stray, to wander. Gable cried seeing the work. He muttered words like bare, honest, confronting but what he meant was death. We all knew that.

Every day brought the exhibition opening closer. And no one else seemed to know that that's when it would all be over. I dreamed of ways to postpone the opening. I thought of bomb scares, setting off the fire alarms. I thought of getting really sick, maybe being run over. Then they'd put it off while I was in hospital. They'd have to put it off. Dad wouldn't let the exhibition open without me.

Nan said, 'It's not up to you to decide, Chrissie. It may not even be up to your father. These things happen in their own time, the way birth does.'

I said, ' I don't know how to say good-bye.'

'You will, when you have to.'

I was sick of it all, too. I hated this waiting. We were all waiting. The exhibition bustle disguised it a little. Mum's work pretended it wasn't happening. School went on, although they must have known by now and no one pulled me up for dreaming in class or spending the lunch hour in the library. I longed for Dad to die so we could all get on with the rest of our lives. At the same time I didn't want him to, I couldn't bear the thought of waking up one day and him not being in the kitchen, taking his first tablet. I couldn't understand how we could go on without his gaunt smile, his fierce eyes.

Some nights Mum came and slept in my room. Or she lay there, rather than sleeping. Sometimes we talked or cried quietly and held hands. I'd go to sleep like that, holding her hand or her holding mine, and when I'd wake up I'd be surprised to find my hand under my cheek.

Other people died, J R R Tolkein, who wrote *Lord of the Rings* died. W H Auden, a poet in England died. Eighteen people died in the Snowy Mountains. They were all old. They were on a pensioners' bus tour of the region. Nan and Badger were pensioners but they kept on living while Dad grew greyer as though the cancer had entered his blood and settled there like ash.

The exhibition was hung. Mum took a week off work so she could drive Dad in and out and help him supervise. Suddenly he seemed more energetic. He talked about the work. Seeing it all in one place made him see it again, he said, and it wasn't bad, not bad.

'If I had more time,' he said but he got out his sketch book anyway and his charcoal and one day he said he felt well enough to show me how to make a lino print. I looked up the word remission in the dictionary and wondered.

I thought of miracles and the power of prayer and those little candles that flickered underneath the statue of Mary in Dee's church. I hadn't lit a candle but maybe someone had, maybe even Dee had, because Dee knew now, everyone did. Maybe Dee's mum lit one, maybe she had asked God on my behalf.

'People,' Mum said carefully the night before the exhibition opened when we were holding hands in our beds, 'people sometimes get a surge of energy before they die. Like a second wind when you're running, or like when you're really tired but you stay up to watch the end of the movie on television and suddenly you're not so tired? As though your body has found a reserve it didn't know it had.'

I didn't want to hear though, and I let my hand drop from hers as though I had just suddenly fallen asleep.

Dad walked into the exhibition opening and everyone there clapped and cheered. If it hadn't been for the coffins, maybe, or the strange x-ray prints, you might not have thought he was sick. You might have thought he was just older than he really was, maybe, or very tired. Nan, Badger and I stayed only a little while. Just long enough to see that everyone did love him so much and to show off my special exhibition dress. Then they took me to dinner with their Italian class to Mama Lucia's and I learnt how to say 'a little more, please' in Italian and I swirled the spaghetti around my fork the way Nan and Badger did. We ate tartuffo icecreams for dessert and the hot splurt of liquid from the centre cherry surprised me so much I got the hiccups and had to drink water backwards.

I stayed the night on a folding up bed at Badger's — well it was really Badger and Nan's but the only bit of Nan you could see were some photos she'd put around the little lounge room and the fresh flowers. The flat was down by the river at West End and the neighbours played some strange hectic music which Badger told me was bazouki music from Greece. Huge cockroaches flew in from the outside trees and Nan wouldn't let anyone step on them. She just swept them outside, and when they'd recovered, they flew right back in.

I was scared one would land on me while I slept so I pulled the sheet up over my head even though Nan said they only came in after the light. I slept well. I knew my father would live. I knew he was in remission. It was a good word, remission. It meant that the cancer had halted, cells were no longer multiplying in his body. The hot spots had retreated and he would have time now to go on with his work. He would look old for a while. I knew that. It would take time for him to recover properly but he would. We had all seen him drinking and laughing last night, forget that he leaned a little on my mother, forget that he couldn't call across the room to a friend, forget the coffins resting together. Remember only that he walked in himself, that a couple of days before he had helped me do a lino print of one of my drawings. Remember that he had eaten breakfast every day for a week.

My father died two days later and I couldn't forgive him.

The Bougainvillea

The lino print we made together hung on my bedroom wall and when I looked at it, I could hear my father's voice.

'Don't forget it costs just as much time and money to make a bad print as it does to make a good one, start small, Chrissie.

We used my frog drawing from my Nature Journal and Dad showed me how to place the drawing on the light box, how to make it simpler, reducing the details to a few bold lines which shouted *frog!* at you, even though bits of it were missing.

I inked up the lino with the sticky printer's ink. I laid the thick damp paper over the block and starting from the top left-hand corner, I finally rubbed the paper all over with the back of a clean wooden spoon and then lifted the paper carefully off the block.

The frog looked as though he was about to leap out of the picture and sometimes that made me cry. My father had shuffled slowly into his death. In the end, the only bit of him which had remained recognisable as Dave, were his eyes, still fiercely blue in the bones of his face.

I didn't know what to do with myself now it was over. I couldn't go to school and sit through the long day there. I couldn't bear the kids watching me. I couldn't bear knowing their fathers were all alive, that their fathers would walk into their homes at six o'clock or half past, shout out, 'where's my girl?' and spin their daughters round in a flurry of love.

I was too angry to go to school. I slouched around, following my mother as she cleaned up the house, crazily washing everything.

'He didn't have the plague, you know,' I shouted at her when I caught her mopping down the studio with disinfectant.

I didn't go to the funeral.

'I don't want to see the coffin,' I said, 'it's just going to be burnt. All that work. He shouldn't have bothered painting it. He shouldn't have wasted his time. He should never have smoked.'

'You need to go,' Mum said, 'otherwise you won't remember he is dead. And what about your flowers?'

'He didn't want flowers. Donate the money to cancer research — look it's in the notebook.'

Mum ignored the notebook I held out, 'You need to see the completion of things. You have to accept it, Chrissie.'

'You can't make me go. You'll have to drag me every step of the way.'

'I don't think she should go,' Nan said, taking the notebook away, 'I think she's seen enough, Rhetta, to remember that he's dead.'

Badger took me to a video arcade instead. While they were burning my father's coffin, I was racing my Space Speedster through enemy territory — dodging alien assassins and asteroids. Every time I shot another one to smithereens, I'd feel a second of relief, as though I had killed part of my own sadness. Beside me Badger flew a Boeing and landed in O'Hare airport in America under difficult weather conditions. He said the Boeing was the hardest to land. When I had written up my name in the top scores, we swapped and I crashed a Cesna in heavy fog.

Gable said we needed to have a memorial service. There were too many people who had known and loved Dad to deny them the right to mourn. Mum said she thought that was a marketing decision on Gable's part. Nan said marketing decision or not she agreed with Gable and why didn't he host it in the gallery?

I didn't want it to be at the gallery because then we'd have to see Mum's coffin all by itself but I knew that's where the service had to be, because that was where Dad was now, mostly, if you didn't count the ashes that were still sitting in a little lacquer box on the mantlepiece because we didn't quite know what to with them.

'Dad wanted a wake,' I told them, 'but he said he didn't want to be mourned. He wanted me to write it in the book, but I didn't. He and Bodhi talked about it. They called it a celebration.'

'That's stretching the point,' Mum said.

'Get this Gable fellow to pay for it,' Badger said, pouring tea, 'he can afford it.'

'Good idea, Badger and Chrissie can do the invitations,' Nan said, 'not much point her going back to school with the year nearly over.'

'Great idea,' Gable beamed when he heard, 'Dave said to watch young Chrissie,' and he rested his hand, with all its winking rings, on my forearm for the briefest moment.

I knew I would do a lino print for the invitation. I loved the bold thick lines the gouging made, those deep troughs the ink missed entirely. I loved the danger in thinking in reverse — what you left untouched was the surface the ink clung to, what you cut away, were the white bits. It was exciting.

Or would be if I could think of what to draw.

'You have to start with something you know,' I could hear my Dad's voice as if he were standing next to me, leaning over my sketch book. '... and I mean know, Chrissie. You have to show me this frog, the one you've seen, jumping out from your paper.'

What did I know? Nothing.

'You have to absorb what you are drawing.

Feel as heavy as that fat little milk jug. Hold yourself as straight as the thin blue vase.'

Mum and Nan left me alone, as though I were a real artist. They bought me sweet corn fritters and glasses of lemonade and sarsparilla cordial. They didn't ask to see the blank pages in my sketch book. Mum piled Dad's art books on the bookcase in my room and I took them down one at a time and looked at them. There was Paris, the pictures my mother had shown me what now seemed like years ago, when we lived in the country and we were all happy. Paris had nothing to do with me, the people dancing belonged to a different time. They were happy, whirling around with each other. Picasso's dove and his little boy and his circus people had nothing to do with me either, although some of them looked thin with sadness, the way I felt.

The women dancers, the show girls with black stockings and flaming hair were beautiful, as were the women coming out of baths, or holding children, but they didn't look like my mother in her waitresses uniform, and the kids didn't look like me, all knobs and angles and shadows.

'When you start out, go for simplicity. Go bold. Don't worry about details, don't get too little about things, Chrissie. The Japanese have a form of painting where you're allowed only one brush stroke — the minute the brush lifts off the paper, the picture is finished. That's simplicity. That's Zen.'

Bodhi came over one day. He was building Nan and Badger coffins now and we had to store them in our shed because they were going to India, to meet a real yoga teacher.

'Just not the sort of thing I want the tenants finding,' Badger explained, 'might freak them out.'

'What about my friends,' I said, 'what about freaking them out?'

So Badger got Bodhi to make a coffin sized cupboard in the shed, with two shelves and a sliding door. 'Oh great,' I said, 'just terrific. That really solves that problem, doesn't it?'

'We can use it for storing things later,' Mum said, 'paint or gardening things, maybe.'

'I'll have it fixed in time,' Bodhi said, 'and it will be so useful. You'll be able to put the table tennis stuff in it.'

He was kind of calm, Bodhi, and because of that I told him.

'I've got two days to do this invitation, Bodhi, and I can't think of anything to draw. Not a thing.'

'You haven't been looking in the right place, Chrissie,' he said, sipping his tea, 'you've made too much of it, it's just a drawing. The main thing is that it tells people when the wake's on, when to come and where. You should just draw what's in front of you now — look, what's wrong with that?' He pointed at the back fence which was sort of sagging under the weight of our purple bougainvillea. Or maybe the bougainvillea was keeping the fence up. It was hard to tell.

I thought of my father walking into the exhibition, leaning on my mother's arm, the small steps they had taken, almost as though he was leading her to an altar, about to give her away. Or she was leading him, and giving him away?

'You're right,' I said, 'you're absolutely right, Bodhi.'

He looked mildly surprised. 'Yeah, okay.' he said. 'Well, good.'

I gouged out the lino so the fence posts were heavier than ours, and more uneven. I didn't worry about all the whorls and knots and lines of wood, just a few to make it clear they were old posts, falling down. I printed that first in black ink, thick and squidgy. Some of the prints smudged, some weren't quite straight but I didn't care, although I was as careful as I could be.

Then I got another block and drew the trailing bougainvillea on it and carefully cut around it. It didn't much look like bougainvillea. In fact it looked a little like a plant from the cover of a science fiction book. It looked as though any minute it might transform into a giant human trap but when I printed it on top of the fence posts, it was okay. It was a plant and it was alive. You could almost feel it growing.

It had to do, anyway, because time was running out. Gable wanted one so he could photocopy it and post them to all the important dealers and collectors and colleagues. Mum wanted some so she could give them out to her friends at the bistro. Nan wanted some for her yoga and Italian classes and I had to send one to Mr Chapman. It didn't matter any more if it was a good print or a bad print, the important thing was that I had done it, and now it was ready.

I didn't expect to enjoy the wake. I walked into the gallery with Mum, Nan and Badger expecting all the prints and Mum's coffin leaning against one wall all by itself, to hurt like I couldn't talk or breathe; instead I felt lightened by them still being there. As though Dad was there, too, not, I knew, just around that pillar or behind that bunch of people all holding wine or beer glasses — but there in the pictures he made.

Some of them would become part of other people's lives, some Mum and I would hang — our favourites. And while he would never again walk into a room, or touch us, or say our names, he had left us his presence. There he was watching — my mother bent over me when I was a baby. There was my father loving us. There he was, in the last year, painting us a dance. It didn't matter that it was on a coffin. And it didn't matter that his own beautiful coffin was ashes, it didn't matter that both my father's coffins would become ashes one day. What mattered was that he had painted us love letters. Sick and dying as he was, he had painted, so we would always know his love.

And there, in the middle of everything, was my poor little fence, my brave bougainvillea, each keeping the other up, framed beautifully in pale wood by Gable, who came towards us now, arms outstretched and hugged us both, not briefly but for the longest time, until I could feel his tears trickling down the back of my neck.

And then we were surrounded by everyone, the way you might be at a surprise birthday party. Even Mr Chapman was there. He gave me a big hug and I smelled a fresh soap smell around him, rather than the old fuggy smell of tobacco. I wondered if he'd given up smoking before the Christmas holidays but he introduced me to his wife, who also gave me a hug and I didn't have a chance to ask because people I didn't even know kept swarming around me, holding me briefly and thanking me for the bougainvillea.

Bodhi gave me a glass of champagne and I drank it straight off even though the bubbles went up my nose and I ate some salmon too, on a little pancake thing and it tasted like smokey tears. I looked at my mother and she looked young, for the first time for months and Nan and Badger were on either side of her, as though there to catch her if she should fall. She won't, I wanted to tell them, we won't now. We'll be okay because he is still here, with us. And that was true and also not true. And we were okay but not always. That's how it is, I suppose.

I took my bougainvillea home even though I didn't hang it on any wall. I took it home because Gable wrapped it up for me and forced it into my arms. And because I knew that an artist would take it and I wanted to think I was artist enough to do what my father would have done. That didn't mean I had to hang it, though. I plastered my walls with pictures of pop singers, a white horse splashing through ocean, copies of my favourite songs and poems written out in my neatest handwriting. I didn't have to hang the bougainvillea and the fence, I was part of them and they were a part of me. I knew everything now about love and death, everything I needed to know.